Pearl
and the Golden Comb

written by
Greta Cleary

illustrated by
Laura Cleary

❦ Table of Contents ❦

You are invited to visit www.castle-tales.com
for free activities and fun resources!

i

for Dr. Hans C. Juvkam-Wold
brilliant and beloved father, grandfather,
teacher, and modern-day Viking

Castle Tales

Science Set 1 - Chemistry
Book 1 - *Pearl and the Golden Comb*
ISBN: 978-1-947926-09-7
First Edition

Printed in the USA

Lilla Press

Chapter 1 - Finding Pearl

In the kingdom of Discovery in a faraway land, Amy was awakened by her little brother's shouts of joy.

"We're getting a puppy!" Micah shouted as he ran down the hall. Amy wanted to go back to sleep, but Micah was right! Today they were getting a puppy!

At breakfast, Mom and Dad were excited too!

"What kind of puppy do you think we'll find at the Royal Animal Shelter?" asked Mom.

"One that is sweet and wants to come home with us," Amy replied.

"One that likes to play and have fun," Micah added.

"Sounds great to me!" Dad smiled. "Better eat up so we can go!"

At the Royal Animal Shelter, Amy and Micah saw many wonderful animals.

Then they looked up to see a girl with long golden hair carrying several shelter animals.

"They're adorable, aren't they?" she said, smiling.

"They sure are!" Amy replied, looking carefully at the golden-haired girl. "You know, you look really familiar."

"I hear that a lot," the girl laughed.

Then to everyone's surprise, a tiny white puppy leaped from the girl's arms, ran to Micah, and jumped into his lap!

"She's so cute!" he exclaimed. "Hey, what's that in her mouth? Is that a...*comb*?"

"Oh, *there* it is!" said the girl. "I keep losing it in my hair."
"Well, I can see why!" Micah blurted out. "Your hair is huge!"

"Micah!" said his mom as his face turned bright red.

"It's okay, he's quite right," the girl laughed. "I should use a different color of comb so I don't keep losing it. But I really like the gold ones."

"Is that comb made of *real* gold?" Amy asked with wide eyes.

"Sure is!" the girl replied. "Gold is my favorite color *and* my favorite **element**!"

"Wait, what? Your favorite *element*? What does *that* mean?" Amy asked, returning the comb.

"Well, elements are the building blocks of the whole world!" the girl said excitedly.

"Do you mean like *toy* building blocks?" Micah wondered.

"Yes, exactly! Everything we can see, hear, smell, touch, or taste is built from one or more elements just like blocks!"

Micah started to imagine a world made of element building blocks...

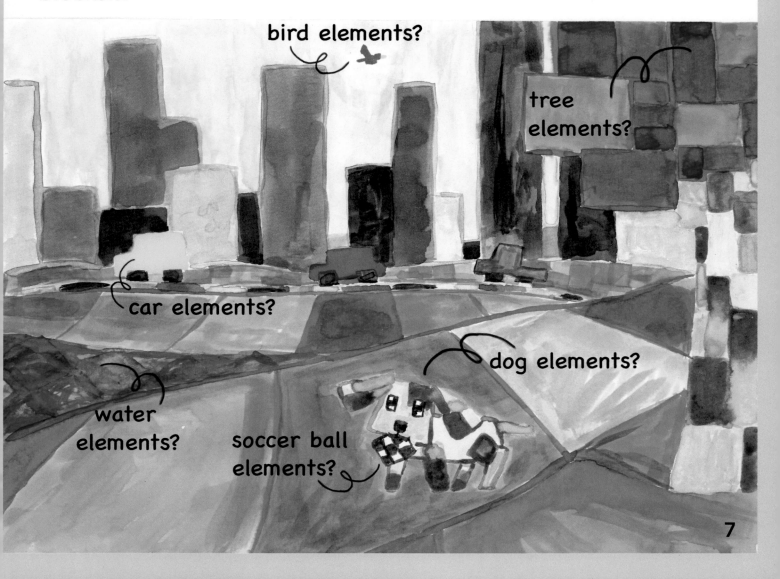

Micah's daydream was interrupted when Amy said, "Okay, so gold is one of the elements, which are the building blocks of the world. But what about water? Is water an element, too?"

"People used to think so. But now we know that water is made of *two different* elements called **hydrogen** and **oxygen**."

"How does it work? Can I make water?" Micah asked, thinking it would be fun to build a lake in his room.

"Well, if you take two hydrogen blocks and one oxygen block, you can build the smallest piece of water possible.

2 hydrogens + 1 oxygen = water!

"But instead of calling it the **'smallest piece'** of water, we call it a **molecule** (MOL-eh-kyool) of water. And *I* think that a molecule of water looks just like a teddy bear head!"

The children laughed, imagining happy water molecules with oxygen faces and little hydrogen ears.

real teddy bear

happy water molecules

"I think building water would be fun!" Micah said excitedly, "But more importantly, what elements do we need to build a chocolate cake?!"

"Well, *that* is a little more complicated," the girl laughed. "Most things we eat, such as apples and chocolate cake, are made of *many* different elements...not just one or two."

Hi! I'm made of **lots** of different elements!

Hey, me too!

Micah was just about to ask what elements he would need to build a rocket ship when Amy gasped.

"Wait a minute! I know who you are!" she looked at the girl. "You have golden hair and a real gold comb, and you're super smart...you're Princess Christina, aren't you?"

"Yes, I am! But you can call me Chris."

"Wow! Well, I'm Amelia, but you can call me Amy."

"And I'm Micah, but you can call me...Micah," he said and everyone laughed.

"But you're a princess. Why do you work here?" Micah asked.

"Well, I'm a volunteer so I come here to help. And I love seeing the animals go to good homes!" Chris said happily.

"I've heard that your castle is enormous and has a room full of treasure! Is that true?" asked Amy.

"Yes, that's true. It's an amazing place to live. You could come and visit and I could show you the treasure room—and your parents could meet my parents. Would you like that?"

"Really?" The children turned to their parents, "Could we?" Their parents smiled and nodded yes.

"Yay! How about tomorrow?" Micah asked excitedly.

"Micah!" his mother exclaimed.

"Sounds great to me, if it's okay with your parents," Chris replied, turning to their parents. They nodded their approval.

As if the puppy could sense their excitement, she started rolling over and doing tricks that made everyone laugh.

"I think this puppy would be perfect for us," Mom said, looking at the family, "What do you think?"

"Yes!" everyone agreed and the children were very excited!

"What should we name her?" Dad wondered.

"Well, she's exactly the color of Mom's pearl earrings. What if we name her Pearl?" Amy suggested.

Micah and their parents agreed completely.

"Congratulations to all of you!" Chris smiled, "When you're ready, you can bring Pearl up to the front desk where the staff members can help you to adopt her."

As Chris gathered the other animals, she said, "In the morning, I'll send a surprise to pick you up to come to the castle. And Pearl is welcome, too!"

Waving goodbye, Chris glanced around the room with a puzzled look before she left.

When the family brought Pearl to the front desk, they saw all the other animals being adopted as well.

"It seems there's a perfect pet for everyone," Mom smiled, looking at all of the happy faces.

Back at home, Amy and Micah played with Pearl until bedtime. Then they all fell asleep dreaming of the next day's adventures.

Chapter 2 - The Castle

Early the next morning, the children heard their mother exclaim, "What is *that* in our front yard?"

Amy ran to her window, but all she could see was a pattern of colors.

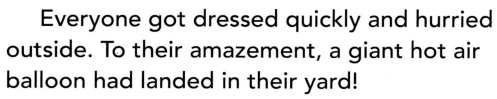

Everyone got dressed quickly and hurried outside. To their amazement, a giant hot air balloon had landed in their yard!

A friendly man in a dark suit stood by the balloon. "Welcome aboard!" he said. "I'm Mr. Bismuth. Ready for a day at the castle?"

"You bet!" exclaimed Micah as they all climbed excitedly into the balloon's basket.

The balloon took them high above the rivers and trees. And they floated over many hills until they saw a beautiful castle sitting high on a cliff by the sea.

17

When they arrived, Princess Chris was at the castle gate. "Welcome!" she said with a big smile. To Amy and Micah's parents she said, "Mr. Bismuth can take you to meet my parents. And I can show Amy and Micah the playroom!"

As their parents went with Mr. Bismuth, Amy and Micah followed Chris into the castle. They climbed up a tall staircase, walked down a long hallway, and finally reached a door with a sign that read "Playroom."

They opened the door to find a huge room full of toys, including a giant ice cream cone slide and three trampolines shaped like jello!

"This is incredible!" Amy exclaimed. "Can we play?"

"Absolutely!" Chris smiled.

Micah raced over to the ice cream slide, Amy ran to the trampolines, and Pearl examined one of the fluffy fruit pillows.

They jumped and played until they were thirsty. So they sat on the trampolines and drank big glasses of water.

Then Chris asked, "Remember how elements are the building blocks of the world? Do you remember what water is made of?"

"Of course! Two hydrogens and one oxygen," replied Micah, surprising the others.

"You're right!" said Chris. "And you need to see something."

Chris walked across the room to a large stone wall, "This is my list of elements!" she explained. "Each stone has an element on it. See the H at the top? Well, H is the secret code for hydrogen. And see the O for oxygen on the other side? Pretty great, right?"

"Yes, but why have an element list on your wall?" Amy asked.

"Because it can do *so* many things! It can even open hidden doors and passageways! Want to find the treasure room?"

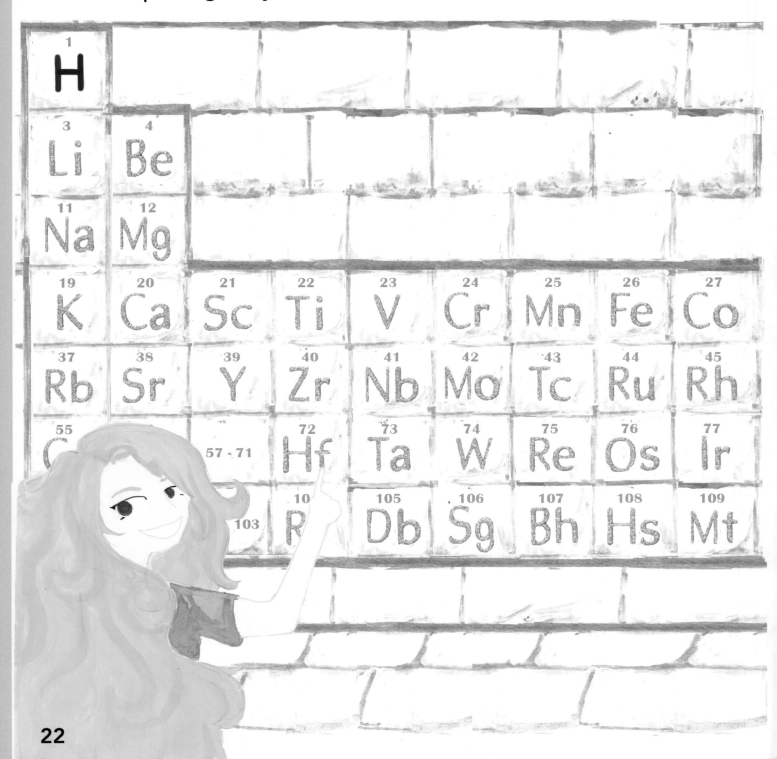

The children nodded in excitement, so Chris replied, "Okay, first we need to find the secret code for gold."

"I don't see a G for gold, "said Amy, looking at the stone list.

"Good point! Some of the secret codes are so old that they come from Latin, which is a very old language. And the Latin word for gold is *aurum* (AWR-uhm), so the secret code is Au."

"I found it!" said Micah excitedly. "Now what do we do?"

							2 He
5 B	6 C	7 N	8 **O**	9 F	10 Ne		
13 Al	14 Si	15 P	16 S	17 Cl	18 Ar		

28 Ni	29 Cu	30 Zn	31 Ga	32 Ge	33 As	34 Se	35 Br	36 Kr
46 Pd	47 Ag	48 Cd	49 In	50 Sn	51 Sb	52 Te	53 I	54 Xe
78 Pt	79 Au	80 Hg	81 Tl	82 Pb	83 Bi	84 Po	85 At	86 Rn
110 Ds	111 Rg	112 Cn	113 Nh	114 Fl	115 Mc	116 Lv	117 Ts	118 Og

"Just press it until you hear a click," Chris explained.

So Micah pressed the Au stone and was surprised when it moved slightly into the wall.

First, they heard the click. Then they heard a low rumble as a hidden door opened to the right of the element list! They ran over to the opening and looked in.

"It's a secret staircase!" exclaimed Amy. "Let's go!"

Pearl led the way down the staircase, following the golden glow from below.

25

When they reached the bottom, they found themselves surrounded by piles of golden treasures!

So they played.

And played.

And played.
Until they were very hungry.

When they returned to the playroom, Micah saw that Pearl was still wearing a tiny gold crown from the treasure room. "Oh, Pearl!" he laughed, "Let's put that back. We don't take things that aren't ours."

The hidden door had closed behind them. So Micah picked up Pearl and walked back to the element wall. But he couldn't remember the secret code for gold.

"Is it Au or Ag to get back to the treasure room?"

"The secret code is Au," Chris smiled. "But we can leave the crown up here. Then Pearl can wear it whenever you visit."

"Thank you! So what would happen if I press Ag?" Micah asked.

"Well, that would open a door to something made of silver. In Latin, silver is *argentum* (ahr-JEN-tuhm). So Ag is the secret code for silver. "

"Oh, that makes sense!" said Amy.

"It *does*?!" the others looked at her in surprise.

"Sure!" Amy smiled. "Mom was born in Argentina. And *she* said it was named for its silver. *Argentum*...Argentina...get it?"

"Oh, I get it!" Micah said happily. "So Ag is the secret code for silver. I'm good with that."

"Excellent!" Chris smiled, "Now should we go eat?"
"Definitely," Amy responded, "But where should we go?"
"To the kitchen, of course!" Chris pointed to the element wall, "Do you see the Cu stone? Go ahead and press it."

Amy walked to the wall and pressed the Cu stone until she heard a click.

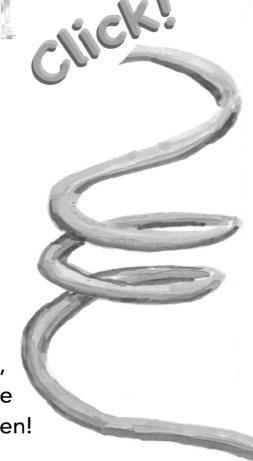

Click!

Suddenly, a trap door opened in the middle of the floor to reveal a giant slide!
"That looks like a water slide ride!" Micah exclaimed. "But aren't we going to the kitchen?"

"We certainly are," said Chris, "This is my shortcut, so let's go!"
"Whee!" shouted Micah as, one by one, they slid down the biggest slide they had ever seen!

At the bottom of the slide, they found a large kitchen full of copper pots, pans, and bowls piled high with food. And they heard their parents talking and laughing in the next room.

31

"Eat anything you'd like," said Chris as she loaded her plate full of fruit.

So they gathered some food and sat down to eat. Then Amy asked, "Why does the Cu stone lead to the kitchen? Is it another secret code from Latin?"

"Yes, it is! The Cu stands for *cuprum* (KYOO-pruhm), which means copper," Chris pointed around the room. "See the copper kettle and all of the copper pots and bowls?"

"Yes, they're really pretty. But most of all, I like that you have a shortcut to the kitchen."

"I think we need one at our house, too!" grinned Micah and they all laughed.

The kitchen was warm and cozy and smelled of freshly baked bread. And Amy didn't know that she was staring at her glass of water until Chris asked if she was okay.

"Yes, I just realized something," she said, turning to her brother, "You know what?"

"What?" he answered, taking a bite of his gigantic sandwich.

"I just figured out why we call water H_2O!"

"Really?" he was surprised.

"Yes! The H_2 means two hydrogens and the O is oxygen! Dad always says we need to drink lots of H_2O."

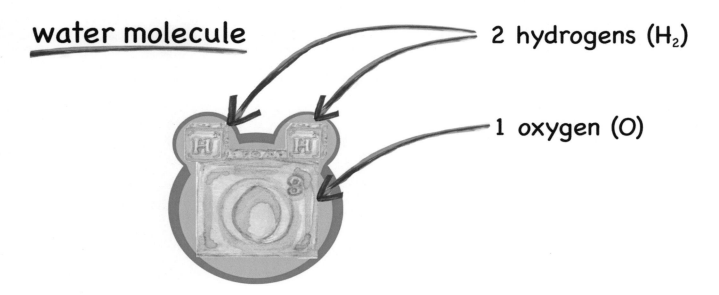

water molecule

2 hydrogens (H_2)

1 oxygen (O)

"You're right! He *does* say that a lot," Micah replied. He looked at Chris, "Can you tell me what a **molecule** is again?"

"Sure! In nature, when at least *two* element blocks join together to make something new, that tiny new thing is called a molecule. So the tiniest piece of water you can find in nature is called a molecule of water."

"Thanks! We've sure learned a lot from you," he said happily.

Amy agreed, "We already know five of the elements, and we've been through two hidden doors!"

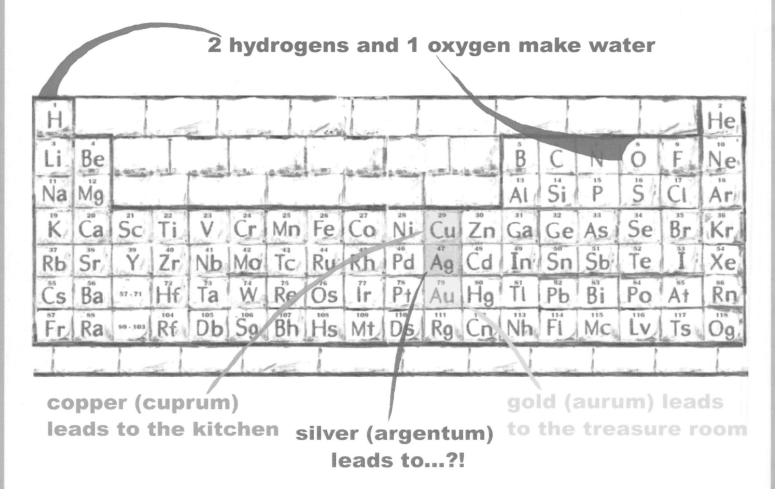

2 hydrogens and 1 oxygen make water

copper (cuprum) leads to the kitchen

silver (argentum) leads to...?!

gold (aurum) leads to the treasure room

"And *I* want to see what the silver stone opens," Micah looked at Chris, "Do *all* of the element stones open hidden doors?"

She laughed, "Many of them do, but others...well, you'll just have to come back and see."

Just then, Amy and Micah's parents walked into the kitchen.

"The king and queen have invited us all to come and visit again soon. Would you like that?" asked Mom.

"Yes!" Amy and Micah exclaimed and Chris was happy.

So the family thanked the princess for a wonderful day and went outside to meet Mr. Bismuth at the balloon.

The sun was setting, and Pearl was excited to go for another ride in the balloon!

As they sailed back through the starry night, Amy, Micah, and Pearl fell asleep dreaming of their next adventure in the castle.

90013072R00022

Made in the USA
Lexington, KY
06 June 2018